The Secret Animal Society

RUTH SYMES would like to have a small dragon
for a pet (or even a well-behaved big one).
She lives in Bedfordshire and when she isn't
writing she can be found by the river walking her
dogs, Traffy and Bella (who are often in the river,
although they've never seen a sea serpent).
Find out more at: **www.ruthsymes.com**

The **Secret Animal Society** series

Cornflake the Dragon
Spike the Sea Serpent
Snowball the Baby Bigfoot

The **Bella Donna** series

Coven Road
Too Many Spells
Witchling
Cat Magic
Witch Camp
Bella Bewitched

The Secret Animal Society

SPIKE
The Sea Serpent

by Ruth Symes

Illustrated by Tina Macnaughton

First published in Great Britain in 2015 by Piccadilly Press
Northburgh House, 10 Northburgh Street, London EC1V 0AT

Text copyright © Ruth Symes 2015
Illustrations copyright © Tina Macnaughton 2015

A CIP catalogue record for this book is available from the British Library.

ISBN: 978-1-84812-446-2

1 3 5 7 9 10 8 6 4 2

Printed and bound by Clays Ltd, St Ives Plc

www.piccadillypress.co.uk

Piccadilly Press is part of the Bonnier Publishing Group
www.bonnierpublishing.com

For lovers of animals (secret or otherwise)
especially Malcolm, Julie, Evie, Mia, Paige, Sophia,
Martin, Devashree, Lewis, Jessie, Eric, Harry, Ben, Dylan,
Morgan, Rose, Lily-Mai, Cameron and Adam

A letter from the author . . .

Dear Reader,

Thank you so much for looking inside this book. I hope you enjoy reading about Spike the Sea Serpent as much as I enjoyed writing about him ☺

Did you know that there have been over 250 reports of lake serpents and water monsters all over the world? Nessie in Scotland, Ogopogo in Canada, Champ in America, Issie in Japan and Selma in Norway are just a few of the better-known ones. I'd love to see a lake monster - so long as it was a vegetarian one like Spike!

The biggest sea-swimming dinosaur was called a Spinosaurus and was more than fifteen metres long from nose to tail . . . and he wasn't a vegetarian. No one's seen one of those swimming in the sea for 95 million years. But if you do spot something unusual and manage to take its picture we'd love to see it at the Secret Animal Society website: www.secretanimalsociety.com

Hope to meet you in another book soon.

Ruth.

CHAPTER 1

Eddie could see out of the minibus windows, but nosey parkers couldn't see in because of the tinted glass. If they had been able to see inside they'd never have believed what they saw: three perfectly ordinary-looking

children, three perfectly ordinary-looking grown-ups, and one not even the least bit ordinary-looking small dragon.

They'd been driving since dawn and it was now evening and getting dark. The roads had become less and less busy as they'd travelled and for the last hour they'd been on a farm track full of potholes with gates to open every now and again.

Eddie glanced over at his nine-year-old twin sister Izzie. She sensed his glance, poked her tongue out at him and crossed her eyes. Eddie grinned. She looked weird when she did that.

Cornflake the dragon had fallen asleep next to the children's father, and was snoring softly. Unlike Dad, who was snoring

4

really loudly with his head back and his mouth open.

Alfonzo, the head of the Secret Animal Society, was driving. He swerved to avoid another pothole but didn't quite manage it and the bus bumped and jolted.

'Huh! What?' said Dad, waking up.

Eddie grinned at him. 'You were snoring, Dad.'

'Not me,' Dad said. He looked down at the dragon beside him. 'It must have been Cornflake.'

'Was you, Dad!' three-year-old Toby said from where he sat on Mum's lap. 'Your nose make loud noise. Cornflake make little ones.'

Cornflake had started off as Eddie and Izzie's school library lizard. He'd only been

5

a few inches long when he was at the school. But when they'd taken him home for the holidays, and let him out of his tank, he'd grown and grown.

Alfonzo had said Cornflake had grown because he was happy to be free of the tank and allowed to wander round the flat, but Izzie was sure it had something to do with how many cornflakes the little dragon had eaten. Whatever the reason, Cornflake was now the size of a large Labrador dog. Although, of course, Labradors couldn't fly or breathe fire.

'Are they all true, then?' Izzie asked Alfonzo.

'Are all what true?'

'The myths and legends about dragons.'

'Well, like most rumours, some of them are and some of them aren't,' Alfonzo said, pushing the green glasses he always wore further up his nose. 'Which ones in particular were you thinking of?'

'That clouds are created by dragons' breath and volcanoes erupt when dragons jump up and down,' Izzie said.

Alfonzo shook his head. 'No those aren't true. And anyway they'd have to be much bigger dragons than your Cornflake if they were!' he chuckled.

'How big will he grow?' Izzie asked.

'Bigger than me already,' said Toby, sounding a bit disappointed.

'It's hard to say, really. But under your care he does seem to have blossomed,'

Alfonzo said. 'He could grow to be very large indeed – or he could stay the same size.'

'Do they eat people?' asked Izzie, thinking of another dragon story. 'I know it's only supposed to be princesses that dragons eat, but what if the writers of those stories made a mistake?'

Toby laughed. 'Eating people - yuck!'

'I heard dragons had crystal skulls,' Eddie said.

'Not true,' Alfonzo said firmly. 'Not true at all. But silly rumours like that have caused a lot of other animals like rhinos and elephants and tigers to be killed. It makes me sick even to think of the damage speculation and misinformation can do.'

Everyone was quiet for a few minutes

as they drove on ever deeper into the now very dark and wild countryside. Then Mum lightened the mood.

'I read somewhere that dragons all have pots of gold,' she said. 'But I don't think Cornflake would be interested in money.'

'Just flakes of golden cereal,' said Dad. 'He'd probably have a collection of those if he could!'

'We learned about a dragon guarding a golden fleece in Greek mythology,' Eddie said. 'Maybe that's how the rumour started.'

'Maybe,' Alfonzo said. 'Stories do change and as they do they often become bigger and stranger. We have some very rare sheep at the sanctuary. Ones that you're highly unlikely to see anywhere else, but their fleece isn't usually gold.'

'SAS SOS, SAS SOS,' the radio crackled. 'SAS SOS.'

Alfonzo spoke into the microphone. 'Alfonzo here. Over.'

'Three reports so far. Marine subject, or possibly subjects, thought to be large and dangerous with lots of tentacles. Top priority. Over.'

'I'll be there ASAP. Over and out,' Alfonzo said.

'Do you need my help?' Dad asked.

'Not just yet,' Alfonzo told him. 'But I might do. We're almost at the sanctuary now. You can get settled in and I'll call if I need you.'

'What does "marine subject" mean?' asked Eddie.

'What's "top priority"?' said Izzie.

'And what's "ASAP"?' Toby wanted to know.

'ASAP means "As Soon As Possible".' Alfonzo told them. 'Top priority means "drop everything and do this instead". And "marine subject", well that means something that lives in the sea, but it could be anything at all from a blue whale to a starfish, a monster to a minnow. I don't know what this creature is, but I'm worried about it having lots of tentacles.'

CHAPTER 2

'Are we nearly there yet?' Toby asked. He was feeling a bit sick and he was bored of being in the minibus.

'We are there,' Alfonzo said. 'And we have been for the last hour.' He swerved as the headlights caught a shape in the road; the animal hesitated for a fraction of a second and then darted away. 'The Secret Animal Society needs a lot of land because we're never quite sure who's coming to stay next,' he went on. 'And because we need to keep it secret of course. That's the most important. We don't want anyone who hasn't been invited to find us and so the sanctuary is very very well hidden. Very hard to spot even from the sky and almost impossible to reach by sea.'

'Good,' Eddie said and Izzie nodded. They wanted the Secret Animal Society animals, like Cornflake, to be safe.

'If you look carefully through the trees you can just see the caretaker's cottage next to the lighthouse.'

Everyone looked and gasped.

'It's beautiful,' said Izzie.

The yellow lights at the windows made the white stone cottage with a thatched roof look welcoming and cosy.

'Our new home,' said Mum, and her voice caught in her throat as she gave Toby a hug.

The cottage was attached to a red-and-white lighthouse that stretched up into the sky.

'Why isn't the lighthouse light working?' Eddie asked.

'It would draw too much attention to us,' Alfonzo said. 'Although we're very secluded here we don't want to risk using the light unless it's an absolute emergency.'

Two people were waiting for them outside the cottage. They smiled and waved as the minibus got closer.

'That's Noah and his wife Beth,' Alfonzo said. 'They're retiring so they'll be leaving once you're settled in.'

Noah, the old caretaker, had a smiling wrinkled face and looked like he was at least a hundred years old. His wife Beth wore her long snowy white hair up in a bun.

'Welcome, welcome,' Noah said, as he shook Dad's and Mum's hands and ruffled Toby's hair, which Toby immediately flattened again with his hands.

'Unfortunately, I have to head off straight away,' Alfonzo said as he took the bags out of the minibus. 'But I'll be back as soon as I can.'

'What's wrong?' Noah asked him.

'There's been a marine sighting that needs investigating,' Alfonzo told him.

'But you've been driving all day,' Mum said. 'You need a break.'

17

Alfonzo shook his head. 'There isn't time. A secret animal needs our help, and the sooner we can help it the better. I can't ignore the call.'

'At least have something to eat,' said Beth. 'I'll make you a sandwich to take with you.'

But Alfonzo shook his head again and hurried back to the minibus. He jumped inside, turned on the engine and speeded away.

'So this is the little dragon I've heard so much about,' Noah said to Eddie and Izzie, who were standing on either side of Cornflake. 'And you are the children who rescued him.' As he smiled his turquoise blue eyes twinkled. 'From what Alfonzo told me, you both are really quite amazing.'

Eddie felt himself start to blush and he was glad it was dark so Noah couldn't see.

'I've been baking,' Beth told Toby. 'I hope you like strawberry cakes.'

'I do!' said Toby, taking Beth's hand.

'Strawberries are his favourite food,' Eddie said, as they went into the cottage.

'Oh good,' Beth smiled and she winked at Mum.

In the kitchen, lying on a hand-knitted woollen blanket, lay a small rainbow-coloured lamb. His head was blue and his body was orange, his legs were yellow, green, pink and cream, his tail was purple and his eyes were a soft chocolate brown.

'Oh,' said Izzie. 'Oh, isn't he lovely?'

She'd never even been this close to a normal lamb before, let alone one of many colours.

The little lamb looked over at them and bleated.

'He's one of three and his mum couldn't care for all her babies at once,' Noah said.

'So we took over,' Beth added. 'He'll go back to his mum and his brother and sister and the rest of the flock once he's strong enough. Probably tomorrow or the next day.'

'Part and parcel of being the new

sanctuary caretaker is having animals that need taking care of in the house,' Noah said to Dad. 'Hope you won't find that a problem?'

'Not a problem at all,' Dad said.

Eddie and Izzie looked at each other and grinned. Having a baby lamb in the house was fantastic!

'Would you like to feed him?' Beth asked Eddie.

'Yes, please,' Eddie said, and put the bottle Beth gave him to the lamb's mouth. It was very hungry and immediately started drinking.

Cornflake made a *humph* sort of sound.

'He's hungry too,' Mum said.

'Oh, the cakes . . . ' Beth said, heading to the oven.

'Actually, he'd probably prefer some cornflakes,' Mum told her. 'If you have any.'

'Yes, we do,' Beth said, opening a cupboard and pulling out a packet.

Cornflake crunched a bowl of cereal while Toby munched on a warm strawberry cake. The  grown-ups sipped tea and Eddie and Izzie took it in turns to feed the rainbow lamb until the milk was all gone and it fell asleep. Then the twins had strawberry cakes too.

'I hope Alfonzo doesn't have too far to go,' Mum said.

'He can't bear for any animal to be in trouble,' Noah said.

'Quite often the sightings turn out to not

be secret animals after all,' Beth told them.
'Only last week there was a report of a foul-
smelling secret animal. Alfonzo went to
investigate and it turned out to be nothing
more than a funny-shaped pile of rubbish.'

'This one's supposed to be large and
dangerous,' Eddie said.

'And there've been three sightings of it so
far,' said Izzie.

She gave her brother a
look. They both secretly
wished that they could have
gone with Alfonzo.

'It's got lots of tenna
things...' Toby said, waving his own
arms about.

'Tentacles,' said Eddie, as Toby sneezed

and Cornflake jumped in surprise and choked on a cornflake.

Toby sneezed again.

'Shall I warm up some honey and lemon?' Beth asked Mum. 'It's very good for stopping colds before they start. Or some thyme tea – that's even better. I've got lots of thyme growing in my herb garden. The tea is a very old remedy. Have you tried it?'

Mum shook her head. 'No, I haven't, but I love the smell of thyme. I grew some in a pot on the rooftop of the flat where we used to live.'

'I'm so glad you like gardening,' Beth said to Mum. 'There's lots to do here. We have to grow a lot of the secret animals' food.'

Toby sneezed again, louder this time.

Cornflake tilted his head to one side and looked at Toby as if he wasn't quite sure what this strange sneezing noise he was making was all about.

'Sounds like you're catching a cold,' Mum said, as she put her hand to Toby's forehead. 'A good night's sleep should help. It's very late for you to be up.'

'Let me show you to your rooms,' Beth said, standing up. 'They're all ready for you.'

Mum picked up Toby and followed Beth out of the kitchen with Eddie and Izzie behind her.

In the flat where they used to live, Eddie, Izzie, Toby and Cornflake all shared one bedroom and Mum and Dad had slept on a sofabed in the lounge, but here Izzie was given her own room.

'Here we are,' Beth said, opening the door to a bedroom with lemon-coloured walls, a bed by the window and a dreamcatcher hanging from the ceiling light. There was a bunch of freshly picked flowers in a little vase on the dresser and some soft fluffy towels on top of the duvet on the bed.

Mum put Toby down and he went over to the bed and pushed it with his finger.

'Nice and soft, Izzie,' he said.

'Thank you,' Izzie said to Beth. 'I love it.'

'You're very welcome,' Beth smiled.

'Where's my room?' said Toby.

'Just next door,' Beth told him.

When they'd gone Izzie went over to the

window and looked out. She was tired from the long journey but she'd still have liked to spot some more of the sanctuary's secret animals before she went to sleep. It was hard to believe this was really now their home.

In the garden below her she saw something that looked a bit like a chicken. It was staring up at the window as she looked out but when it saw Izzie it waddled quickly into a bush.

Izzie kept staring at the spot where it had disappeared, but it didn't come out again.

'There's enough bedrooms for everyone to have one of their own,' Beth said to Toby and Eddie, as she opened the door of the room next to Izzie's.

Toby went inside and then came out again and shook his head. 'Want to be with

Eddie,' he told Beth, as he took hold of Eddie's hand. He'd never had a room of his own before. Cornflake put his paw in Toby's hand. 'Cornflake with us too.'

'Then you'd better have this one,' said Beth, opening the door opposite. Inside was a larger room with four beds in it.

'Perfect!' Toby said flopping down on his bed. 'Nice and bouncy.'

Cornflake hopped up onto the bed beside him.

Eddie went to the window and looked out, just like Izzie had done. Far off in the distance he heard something – he'd no idea what – roar.

CHAPTER 3

Eddie and Izzie both woke at exactly the same time the next morning.

But both of them smelled different things. Izzie woke to the aroma of pancakes cooking. Eddie could smell hash browns sizzling.

Toby woke a few minutes later feeling a little stuffed up. He could smell strawberry waffles. Cornflake was already awake and downstairs eating cornflakes when all three came into the kitchen.

'He really does like them, doesn't he?' Beth said.

'Never met a cereal-crunching dragon before,' said Noah, as he watched Cornflake eating.

'He'll eat other food too,' Izzie said. 'But cornflakes are his favourite.'

Toby sneezed again. His eyes looked very red and he wasn't feeling happy.

'Throat scratchy,' he said, as he wiped his nose with his hand.

'Looks like you've caught a nasty cold,' said Mum, giving him a tissue.

'Would you like to see the herb garden after breakfast?' Beth asked Mum. 'We could give the thyme tea cold cure a try.'

Mum looked doubtfully at Toby and the strawberry waffle he was pushing round his plate with a fork.

'Green stuff is very good for you,' she said.

But Toby pulled a face. 'I like strawberry jam sandwiches,' he said.

Beth smiled.

'Well, I think it'd be a good idea to visit the herb garden,' Mum said. 'Thyme tea could be just the thing, especially with a spoonful or two of honey in it.'

'Come on, Cornflake,' Toby said, as Mum took his hand and they headed out of the kitchen with Beth.

'I'd better show you your office,' Noah said to Dad when he'd finished his tea and toast.

'Office?' said Dad. 'I didn't know I had an office.'

'It's in the lighthouse next door,' Noah told him.

Eddie gulped down the last of his hash brown potatoes covered in tomato ketchup. He and Izzie had never been in a lighthouse before so when Dad and Noah stood up they went with them.

'Long way up,' Eddie said, as he stared up to the top of the lighthouse. It was taller than two houses stacked on top of each other – maybe even taller than three houses.

'Two hundred and sixty-nine steps to the top,' Noah told him.

'That's a lot,' sighed Dad. 'Alfonzo didn't mention the steps.'

'Don't worry, you'll soon get used to them,' Noah said. 'I've been up and down them every day for the past forty years and it's done me no harm at all.'

He opened the door and they went inside.

At the bottom of the lighthouse was a round room with pictures of some of the sanctuary's secret animals and a map on the wall.

'Your office,' Noah said.

They'd only just gone inside it when the phone on the wooden desk started ringing and Noah gestured at Dad to pick it up.

'Hello?'

'It's Alfonzo.'

'How are you getting on? Did you find the secret animal?' Dad asked Alfonzo. He pressed the loudspeaker button so everyone could hear.

'No, the creature was gone by the time I got there. But let me give you the co-ordinates so you can mark where it's been seen on the map. We might be able to work out where it's heading.'

Alfonzo read out a series of numbers. Noah pulled open a drawer full of drawing pins and Dad took one out and stuck it to the map in the place where Alfonzo had just told him.

'Any more clues what it might be?' Eddie asked, excited to discover what it was.

'No – but it's most likely a giant squid,' Alfonzo replied. 'Although it might be the much larger colossal squid, of course. Both fascinating animals but not secret animals. If it turns out to be a Hydra, though...'

'What's that?' asked Izzie.

'A multi-headed water dragon.'

'Have you ever seen one of those?' Eddie asked.

'No, and I'd rather not,' Alfonzo said. 'And I don't much fancy meeting a Skylla, either, if that's what it turns out to be.'

'What's a Skylla?'

'A sea-monster that has many legs, and long grasping necks with dog heads on the ends of them. Anyway I'd better be going. I'll call again as soon as I have more information.'

'Be careful,' Noah said.

'I will,' Alfonzo said, and he rang off.

'This mission sounds very dangerous,' said Dad.

'Alfonzo's done this at least a hundred, maybe even two hundred, times before,' Noah told him. 'He knows what he's doing.'

He tapped the cover of a very large,

ancient-looking, leatherbound book in the centre of the desk. 'Don't forget to log the sighting in here.'

Eddie and Izzie looked over Dad's shoulder as he turned the thick creamy coloured pages of the book. It listed all the animals that had ever lived at the sanctuary and there were helpful handwritten notes from previous caretakers about each of them.

'The fire bat prefers moonbeams to sunbeams...'

'Never wake a sleeping yeti...'

'The log of sightings is at the back,' Noah said. 'We record them on the computer too, these days, of course. But investigating sightings isn't usually the caretaker's job.

The Yeti
Habitat Mountainous, Alpine
Forest and glacial areas.
~ DO NOT WAKE A SLEEPING YETI ~
Description A cross between
a Leopard + bear + an
old man. Its long beard
often earns it the name
'The old man of the mountain
SIZE 6-8ft tall, 80-110kg

EYES - GREEN
+ AMBER
FUR - WHITE
TO GREY

FEMALE ARE *
THE MOST
DANGEROUS!!

Last Sighted: Himalayas
Status: Endangered!!

Your job is looking after the animals that
are at the sanctuary already.'

Dad nodded.

'This book helps to keep a register of
who's here and who's gone, as well as secret
animals that have been sighted elsewhere,'
Noah went on. 'Some of them I don't see for
years, other than an occasional glimpse. If it
wasn't for the food I put out being eaten you
wouldn't even know many of them are here
at all. But that's good – this is their home,

not a zoo, and they're free to wander about as they like, or stay hidden if they want to. Many of them are frightened of people with good reason. Human beings aren't always kind to animals – whether they're secret ones or not.'

'Do any of the secret animals ever leave the sanctuary?' Eddie asked.

'Not often,' Noah told him. 'Although I still miss Spike.' He looked sad.

'Who's Spike?' Eddie asked.

'Alfonzo said he was related to something with a funny name – now what was it? A ple . . . plesio . . . plesioursaurus – that's it. He used to live in the turquoise saltwater lake.'

Eddie and Izzie's mouths fell open.

'A dinosaur! We've got a dinosaur here?'

'A real-life water dinosaur?'

'Like the Loch Ness Monster?'

'Well, sometimes they're called serpents or monsters but Spike wasn't a monster,' Noah said.

'I thought the Loch Ness Monster was just a myth,' said Eddie.

'And that's just what the Secret Animal Society would like you to think,' Noah told him.

'So is the Loch Ness Monster really real?'

'The truth is I don't know for sure. Nessie's a freshwater or lake serpent and she's not the only one we know of. There's also Chessie in Chesapeake Bay in America as well as Cressie, Tessie, Bessie and Ogopogo in different lakes dotted around the USA and Canada. Not forgetting Issie...'

'There's a sea serpent with my name!' squeaked Izzie, and she grinned at Eddie.

'Yes, only it's spelled a little differently,' said Noah. 'And there's also one called Kusshi in another of the Japanese lakes, and Selma in Norway. Lake monsters have been seen just about all over the world.'

'Are they all plesiosaurs?' Izzie asked.

'We don't know for sure. But they're probably related to them at least,' Noah said.

'And they're all real?' said Eddie.

Noah shook his head. 'We don't know that either. But Spike, well Spike was definitely real. I just hope he's still out there somewhere.'

Dad and Izzie gave each other a look as Noah pulled his wallet from his pocket and took a Polaroid photo of Spike from it.

Spike!

'Managed to capture him one day on my camera,' he said.

Spike was obviously very special to Noah.

'Maybe Spike will come back,' Izzie said.

But Noah shook his head. 'It's been more than thirty years since I last saw him.' He gave a loud sigh and then said, 'Enough of reminiscing. Let me show you the rest of the lighthouse.'

At the bottom of the stairs, Noah grasped the handrail and they followed him up the spiral staircase.

CHAPTER 4

'Ninety eight ... ninety nine ... one hundred!'
Eddie counted, as they climbed upwards.

'Only one hundred and sixty-nine left to
go,' Noah said cheerily.

'The coast around here was known as

Shipwreck Shore a hundred years ago because of all the ships that used to get stuck on the rocks. We still find flotsam and jetsam along the beach. No modern wrecks, though. Shipwreck Shore is too secluded for anyone to sail this way nowadays and its olden days name's been forgotten so it doesn't get marked on any maps.'

Noah didn't seem to be getting out of breath at all but everyone else was. They passed another two round rooms as they went upwards. Soon no one besides the old caretaker had any breath left for talking.

'You can see the whole of the sanctuary and far out to sea from the top of the lighthouse – you might just see the unicorns

playing or even a woolly mammoth or two,'
Noah said.

That was enough to get Eddie and Izzie
climbing faster again.

'At last,' Eddie gasped as they reached
the room at the top. It had six windows and
six telescopes for looking out of them.

Now they were at the top Izzie could see
that much of the sanctuary was covered

by woodland and mountains so the secret animals had somewhere to hide if a plane flew over the grounds. It was so big that she couldn't even see all the way to the ends of the sanctuary from up high.

'Do planes fly over here?' she asked.

Noah shook his head. 'Not that I've ever seen, other than our own secret animal helicopter, of course.'

'Have you ever had trespassers here?' Dad asked.

But Noah shook his head again. 'Why would we? This place is so hard to find that no one would just stumble across or drive into it by mistake. We're not on any flight-path and the coastline's too dangerous for anyone to want to sail past.

'I can see an elephant – a baby elephant with its mum,' Izzie cried.

'That's not quite an elephant – or at least not a modern-day one,' said Noah, and he winked at Eddie, who was almost bursting with excitement because he knew what the almost-but-not-quite-an-elephant had to be.

'It's a baby woolly mammoth!' he said, and Noah nodded.

'There's quite a few of them living here nowadays. The adults are very wary of people but the young ones aren't quite so shy and will come over to say hello and eat an apple. They're very partial to apples.'

Izzie looked over at Eddie and she knew they were both thinking exactly the same thing. Feeding an apple to a baby woolly mammoth would be just about the best thing in the whole world.

Then Eddie had a worrying thought.

'The mammoths are pretty big to hide,' Eddie said. 'I know you said no planes ever fly over here but what if a microlight or even a hot air balloon or something went astray and ended up flying past and saw them?'

'Hasn't happened so far,' Noah said.

Dad looked at Eddie. 'Remember when we went to the wildlife park and saw the elephants?'

Eddie nodded.

'What happened when they went in amongst the trees?'

'We could hardly see them,' said Eddie.

'They blended right in,' Izzie said.

'Same thing for mammoths – and most of the other animals here,' Noah told them. 'And the thing about people is, as you found with your dragon, most of them only believe in what they know to be real. So even if a low-flying plane strayed off course, and someone saw a herd of unicorns, they'd probably just convince themselves that it was a herd of wild horses instead.'

Izzie looked through the telescope facing out to sea and saw waves crashing onto the shore. There were so many rocks out there that it would be very hard for a boat to steer its way through them even with the lighthouse to show the way.

'I used to spend hours looking out of that telescope, willing Spike to come home,' Noah said. 'I'd say he was my favourite of all the sea serpents. Not that we've ever had that many visiting us. Not like the merfolk and sea lions; we get plenty of those. But Spike, well, he had more of a personality than most.'

'Sealions aren't mythical,' Eddie said, pressing his eye to the telescope that looked back inland, all the way across the valley to the brooding black mountains on the horizon. 'I've seen lots of sealions at the aquarium.'

'Not sealions – sea *lions*,' Noah told him. 'Their manes look like seaweed and they have a fearsome roar.'

Eddie grinned. He'd like to see one of those. But maybe not up close.

'I can see Spike's lake,' he said, as the telescope lens showed a beautiful sparkling turquoise lake in the middle of the sanctuary, bordered by trees and rocks.

'Come and see this,' Dad said, looking through another telescope. 'There's a waterfall just beyond the herb garden at the back of the cottage! It flows into a river that winds its way to the sea.'

Izzie went to look. Far down below them she could see her mum and Beth in the herb garden. Toby and Cornflake were playing on the lawn at the front of the cottage with the toy tractor and trailer that Toby had been given for his birthday. Cornflake was really too big to fit in the trailer any more but he'd somehow managed to squeeze himself into it.

Toby was struggling to move the tractor along by pushing it with his legs.

'This way Cornflake . . . *atchoo*!'

Suddenly Cornflake made a cawing sound, flapped his wings and flew upwards. He flew off, swooping over the grassy fields, wings flapping wildly, towards the turquoise lake and back again to a laughing – and sneezing

– Toby. Toby moved the tractor forward so Cornflake could make a perfect landing on the trailer.

'It's great, isn't it?' Eddie said to Izzie.

'It's perfect,' Izzie replied. 'And all thanks to Cornflake. Without him we'd never have met Alfonzo and Dad wouldn't have the caretaker's job here.'

Eddie pressed his eye to the glass of the fifth telescope. He saw three black specks in the sky heading towards them, getting larger by the second.

'Wh-what's that?' he said, as he pointed at what now looked like three giant-sized birds, only not exactly birds because there was something different about them. Their wings seemed to beat angrily at the air.

Eddie's heart started thumping very fast.

No one needed to use the telescopes to see them any more. They were huge.

'They look like . . . they look like . . . ' Izzie said, as she squinted to see better in the sun's glare, 'they look like dragons!'

'Well, I never!' said Noah. 'They usually stay in the mountains. And I've never seen three of them before.'

These dragons weren't the size of a Labrador like Cornflake. These dragons were the size of lorries.

They all watched as Toby put his hands up to his eyes as the shadows of the dragons fell over him.

'Uh-oh.'

As the dragons swooped down they gave a cry and bursts of flame came from their mouths.

Izzie was terrified for her little brother.

'Look out!' she screamed. 'Toby – look out!'

CHAPTER 5

Eddie, Izzie, Dad and Noah raced down the lighthouse staircase, desperately trying to reach Toby before the dragons did.

'Toby!' Izzie screamed, as Mum charged across the lawn and scooped Toby up in her arms as the huge dragons circled around them.

Cornflake wasn't frightened of the larger dragons. Not one little bit. He cawed and flapped his much smaller wings excitedly and then flew up into the sky to join them.

'Cornflake, come back!' cried Toby, struggling to break free of Mum.

Izzie and Eddie watched in horror as Cornflake flew across the sky with the big dragons, heading towards the black mountains, until at last they couldn't see him any more.

'He's gone,' sobbed Toby, as Mum hugged him to her tightly. 'You're squishing me,' he told her. But she didn't release her hold and she planted kisses all over his hair, which Toby didn't like much.

'He'll come back,' said Izzie, swallowing to get rid of the lump in her throat. She didn't know if Cornflake was coming back or not. What if the big dragons hurt him? He was so much smaller than they were. He could only breathe small puffs of smoke and occasionally a flame. Not great bursts of fire like the big dragons could. What if they ate him?

'I bet he'll be back in a minute,' Eddie told Toby. 'He came back when he went away before.'

As he said the words he knew this time was different. This time there were other dragons involved.

Izzie looked at her brother. Cornflake could come back. But would he? The little dragon was free to go where he liked now and the other dragons were the same species as him, although much bigger. He might prefer to live with dragons than humans.

She didn't want him to leave. No one did.

'We have to let him go if he wants to,' Dad said. 'The big dragons didn't force him to go with them, he chose to do so. Cornflake has to be free to live his own life just like all the other animals here.'

'Fine dragons, those are,' Noah said. 'Could be hundreds and hundreds of years old.'

'I don't care how old they are! They could have killed Toby,' Mum said. She was really, really upset. So angry she was almost exploding.

Toby's mouth opened wide in surprise. 'No, they couldn't,' he said. '*Atchoo*! They didn't come to see me they came to see Cornflake. *A-a-a-atchoo*!'

'We don't know that, Toby,' Mum said. 'And even if they did come just for Cornflake, you could have been injured by them. They could have knocked you over or set you on fire. You could have been eaten!'

'None of the secret animals have ever injured or harmed anyone here,' Noah said mildly.

'But they're WILD animals,' Mum went on, ignoring Noah. 'Even if they're secret ones. Just because they haven't hurt anyone yet doesn't mean that they never will.' She looked over at Dad. 'Alfonzo's headed off on a mission to find something large and DANGEROUS. Even he said he didn't want to see a Hydra or a Skylla. I think maybe coming here wasn't such a good idea after all. Not with the children.'

'But, Mum . . .' said Izzie.

'We love it here,' said Eddie.

Mum only shook her head. 'I don't want you getting hurt,' she said. 'Alfonzo should have warned us. I'm sorry but I've made up my mind. We can't stay here after all. Pack your bags – we're leaving.'

'But what about Cornflake?' wailed Toby.

'What about all the other animals here that need us?' Eddie said.

'Let's not be hasty,' Dad said. 'Remember how excited we were to come here? And the cottage is wonderful, much better then the flat. What would I do for a job if we leave? And where would we live? Just give it a chance. Give it a month and then decide?'

Mum shook her head.

'A week then?'

Mum sighed. 'A week – but if one more thing like those dragons happens we're packing up and leaving immediately. Agreed?'

She looked at each one of them sharply.

'Agreed,' they all said, although none of them really did.

'But you have to stay,' Beth said. 'Our bags are all packed and we're leaving.

67

Who'll look after the animals if you go too?'

'The cottage comes with the job, and as we're retired . . .' Noah's voice drifted off and he wiped his nose on his handkerchief.

'It's yours now,' said Beth. She bit her bottom lip. Neither Noah or Beth looked happy about going.

Mum looked at Dad. Dad looked at Mum. The cottage had more than enough space for everyone.

'There's lots of room here . . .' said Mum.

'We could do with being shown the ropes . . .' said Dad.

'I certainly wouldn't feel safe unless you were both here too,' Mum went on.

'Please stay,' said Izzie.

'We like you,' Toby said, taking Beth's hand.

'Are you sure we wouldn't be in your way?' Beth said to Mum and Dad. 'We thought you'd probably want to put your own stamp on the place.'

'Not a bit of it.'

'It is very hard to leave here,' Noah said. 'Breaks my heart just to think of it.'

'Then stay!' they all said together.

Noah looked at Beth and Beth looked at Noah.

'We'd love to,' they smiled.

'Then that's agreed.'

'A week,' Mum reminded everyone. 'We're giving it a week's trial and then we'll talk about it again.'

Dad nodded. But they all knew a week was a very long time and anything could happen between now and the end of it.

Izzie looked up at the sky as they went back into the cottage. She hoped Cornflake was all right wherever he was. She hoped he'd come back soon.

'And as for you, Toby,' Mum said, 'you've been sneezing ever since we got here and I'm not sure even the thyme tea is helping.'

Toby wiped his hair where Mum had been kissing it. 'Yes it is,' he said quickly. 'My cold's nearly gone already. More get-better-tea, please, Beth.'

'With pleasure,' Beth said, and she poured him another cup and added two spoonfuls of honey to it.

'This is my third one,' Toby told Izzie and Eddie. 'Thyme in my tummy is yummy yummy yummy!'

CHAPTER 6

SAS

Cornflake still hadn't come back when Alfonzo called an hour later and Eddie answered the phone.

'Shall I get Dad?' Eddie asked. 'He's in Noah's workshop.'

73

'No, I haven't got time to wait. There's so many conflicting reports coming in at the moment it's hard to know what's fact and what's fiction. The most likely explanation is still that the animal's a giant squid or a whale, but I'm investigating every sighting just in case.'

Alfonzo gave Eddie more co-ordinates to mark on the map with drawing pins.

'There's a lot of ocean out there and every time I reach an area the animal's been seen in it's gone. No one seems able to agree on exactly what it was they saw. It's some sort of sea creature with a massive amount of tentacles, though,' Alfonzo said. 'Everyone agrees on that. Although how many tentacles and how big and how dangerous it is – well,

that isn't so certain. Fortunately, everyone's story is different so the media hasn't picked up on it yet. All the Secret Animal Society needs is for someone to capture it on camera and we'll be in big trouble.'

'We could help,' Eddie said. 'Izzie and me – we'd like to help.'

'I know you would,' Alfonzo told him. 'But at the moment there's nothing you can do.'

Eddie put the phone down and went to join Izzie who was in the kitchen. She was feeding the rainbow lamb, sat next to its basket on the grey stone floor that ran throughout the cottage.

'Isn't it cold down there?' Eddie asked her.

'I don't mind,' Izzie said. Not if it meant she got to feed the lamb.

'Cool underfoot in the summer and warm in the winter,' said Beth. 'Also good for mopping up any little accidents,' she added, looking over at the rainbow lamb.

Eddie grinned because he knew

Beth was more than happy to have the lamb staying with them.

Izzie had only just finished feeding the lamb when there was a noise at the back door. The lamb trotted over to it and bleated at the door from the other side.

'It's his mum,' Beth said. 'Telling him it's time to come back to the flock.'

Eddie opened the door and the lamb bounced out and rubbed his head against his mother. It bleated over and over with happiness. The pair of them looked back at Izzie, Eddie and Beth, almost as if they were saying thank you. Then they trotted off out of the garden towards the pasture where the other rainbow sheep and lambs were grazing.

'Time to get the rest of the sanctuary animals' food ready,' Beth said, and they headed over to the herb garden to join Toby and Mum who were already there.

At the entrance to the garden there was a wooden figurehead shaped like a mermaid from a boat that had been shipwrecked long ago.

'I like to think of her as my garden's guardian,' Beth said. 'Noah put her there because he thought she might act a bit like a scarecrow and scare away

the birds and rabbits that eat their way through my plants. But it didn't work. I think she's too friendly-looking.'

'Maybe she needs a scarf or some floaty material around her to make her look like she's moving. That would scare them,' Eddie said.

'I don't mind them coming really,' Beth said. 'We've got plenty of food for everyone.'

'Mum says she's got green fingers,' Toby said, as he watched his mum digging. 'But they don't look green.'

'It just means she's good at making plants grow,' Beth told him.

'You good too,' Toby said, staring at the garden. 'Big cabbages.'

'They do look a lot like cabbages, don't

they?' Beth smiled. 'But they're not quite the same. That's sea kale – the leaves are thicker than cabbage leaves. Delicious when it's fried. You'll have to give it a try.'

Toby didn't look too sure about that.

'Sea kale used to be Spike's favourite food,' Noah said as he loaded the trailer. 'He could never get enough of it. Luckily there's lots growing all along the shore.'

'What was Spike like?' Eddie asked.

'Was he scary like the dragons?' said Izzie. She was worrying about Cornflake still. But she couldn't forget how he'd seemed happy to go off with them. He'd wanted to go with the big dragons. But she wanted him to come back.

'No,' Noah laughed. 'Spike was the most

scaredy-cat serpent you could meet. He'd jump at the sight of his own shadow. I stumbled across him one day singing to his reflection in the lake. Such a sad song.'

'He must have been lonely,' Izzie said.

'Yes, that's what I thought too. He had the most beautiful voice. It was a sort of deep hum but much more than that. He gave a shriek when he saw me, though, and jumped into the lake with a giant splash. Wasn't long after that that I noticed he wasn't in the turquoise lake any more. Always blamed myself a bit,' Noah said. 'Thought maybe me giving him a fright scared him away . . .'

'Oh no,' said Dad. 'I'm sure it wasn't your fault.'

'That wouldn't happen,' said Izzie, trying to reassure him. But Noah only shook his head.

'I wouldn't like to be the reason he left here,' he said. 'The lake's saltwater and not far from the sea. He could be anywhere out there now.'

'He'll come back,' said Toby. 'Like Cornflake will too.'

But no one looked very sure about that.

'What else do you grow?' Izzie asked Beth, changing the subject.

'Herbs and fruits, and of course seaweed.'

'Seaweed in the garden?' said Toby.

'No, I harvest some seaweed from the shallow rock pools of the sea,' Beth told him. 'Never too much and I'm always very careful because of the tiny sea horses and crabs and prawns that live amongst it. Plus I also tie ropes between bits of the olden day ship-wrecks in the tidal water along the shore and the seaweed grows on those too.'

'I'd love to have a go at growing seaweed,' Mum said and Beth smiled.

Once all the food for the animals was ready it was time to deliver it.

'One minute,' Izzie said, and she ran back into the kitchen and came out with a box of cornflakes. 'Might need these.'

'Good idea,' said Eddie.

Dad took corn to the golden-egg-laying geese and singing chickens. Noah drove out to the pasture with Izzie and Eddie on a three-wheeled scooter with a trailer behind it.

'The three-wheeler's better for uneven ground like this,' he said.

As they drove around the sanctuary they looked for Cornflake and called out his name.

'Do you think he's OK?' Izzie asked Noah.

Noah nodded. 'Yes I do. He looked very

happy to meet those other dragons. It's probably been years and years since he saw another one.'

Eddie looked at Izzie. He did understand that it must all be very exciting for Cornflake but it was so hard not having him around. Before they came to the sanctuary they'd had to keep Cornflake a secret. He could only fly in their small flat or up on the roof at night when it was dark. But here there was so much to explore and their little dragon was free, free to go wherever he liked.

But Eddie still worried about him.

'Cornflake!' he called, as he looked all around him. 'Cornflake!

Izzie shook the cereal box in case

the sound of his favourite food tempted him back. But the little dragon didn't return.

'Look!' said Eddie.

Ahead of them was a herd of unicorns nibbling on grass and playing in the sunshine. But they scattered at the sound of the three-wheeler's motor.

'Oh,' said Izzie, disappointed.

'They'll be back,' Noah reassured her. 'Once it's quiet.'

Izzie and Eddie threw out hay for the unicorns from the back of the trailer.

'Can you see any?' Izzie asked. She wanted them to come back and eat the food.

'Nope.'

'They're out there,' Noah told them. 'Watching.'

'Food!' Izzie shouted into the air but still none of the unicorns appeared to eat the hay.

'I wish all the animals would come out so we could see them properly,' said Eddie.

'They will once they get used to you,' Noah said. 'Give them time. You'll be amazed how many there are living here. Fifty-four different species that are supposed to be either extinct, or never even to have existed, according to my last count.'

Izzie told him about the chicken-parrot she'd seen.

'I think it lives in the bush under my bedroom window.'

'That's Doris our dodo,' Noah told her. 'Friendliest bird at the sanctuary once you get to know her – try feeding her a bit of bread. She loves sandwiches. I'm hoping one day Alfonzo will find another one so Doris will have a friend.'

'But I thought all dodos were extinct?' Eddie said.

Noah raised an eyebrow. 'Did you now?' he said.

'And that's just what the Secret Animal Society would like me to think, isn't it?' Eddie grinned.

'Well, it certainly makes keeping them safe a lot easier,' said Noah.

They poured some wet mushy food and vegetables into a long trough and then Noah put two fingers in his mouth and made a loud shrill whistling sound.

The next moment there was a squeal of excitement and nine pigs, big ones and little ones, brown, black, and mottled colours, came flying through the sky and swooped down to the trough to eat their dinner.

'Can your dad whistle?' Noah asked Eddie and Izzie.

'Not as loudly as you can,' Eddie told him.

'I can whistle but not like you,' said Izzie. 'Not through my fingers.'

'You just need a bit of practice. I'll show you how,' Noah said.

'Will you show me too?' asked Eddie.

Noah nodded. 'Happy to.'

'Do the flying pigs always come when you whistle?' Izzie asked.

'Yes,' Noah told her. 'I'd know there was something really wrong if they didn't.'

CHAPTER 7

SAS

When they got back to the lighthouse the phone was ringing again.

'Are Eddie and Izzie there?' Alfonzo asked Dad. 'I need their help, and yours too. Put me on speaker phone.'

'How can we help?' Eddie asked.

'There's been a report of a giant twenty-tentacled squid off the coast not far from you. A party of school children were on a day-trip at sea when they saw it. The boat they're on should be back in an hour. You've just got time, if you leave right now, to get to the port and mingle with the children to find out what they've seen. I'll join you as soon as I can, but it's going to take me longer to get there.'

'Where are you going?' Mum asked, as Izzie and Eddie hurried out to the SAS van with Dad.

'To be SAS detectives,' Eddie said.

'I don't want them in any danger,' Mum told Dad.

'They won't be,' Dad reassured her. 'All we're doing is asking some children and teachers who saw the sea creature what it was like.'

'OK,' Mum said. 'As long as they're safe.'

'I want to go too,' said Toby. But Mum said he couldn't.

Dad drove along the dirt track as fast as he dared but not too fast because they didn't want to injure any of the animals. Finally they left the sanctuary via the tree- and bush-covered gate. No one, who didn't know the truth, would ever have guessed what lay behind it.

'Hurry, Dad,' Izzie said. She didn't want them to get there too late.

But Dad kept to the speed limit.

'A speeding ticket's the last thing we need,' he warned her.

They reached the port just as the boat was coming in. But they weren't the only ones there to meet it. The local press and coastguards were in attendance and so were the police.

'Sorry, sir, no one's allowed in until

statements have been taken,' one of the police officers told Dad, as he blocked his way.

'But . . .'

'Shouldn't be long, sir. There's a bench over there to wait on.'

There was nothing Dad could do but sit on the bench and wait.

While the police officer was busy speaking to Dad, Eddie and Izzie were able to slip inside. The other adults presumed they were children from the boat.

It was very noisy inside the terminal and everyone wanted to talk about what they'd seen.

Some of the children had been frightened, but most of them were excited now it was over. All of them seemed to have seen something a little bit different to each other.

'It was huge and it had these giant-sized pointed teeth like shark's teeth,' one girl told Izzie.

'Did you see its shark's teeth?' Eddie asked a boy standing near her.

'Teeth? It didn't have teeth, it had a long

forked tongue like a snake,' the boy said.

'Its eyes looked right through me,' a different girl with her hair tied in a plait told them.

'It had scales,' said someone else.

'It had wings . . .'

'It didn't. That's rubbish.'

'It had webbed feet.'

'It didn't have any feet, just a tail.'

'Everyone's telling us something different,' Eddie whispered to Izzie.

'No story's the same,' said Izzie. But they questioned everyone they could anyway.

'The little one made this weird sound . . .' said a boy with long hair.

'There was more than one creature, then?'

Eddie asked. No one else had said there were two.

The boy nodded. 'Might have even been three.'

But that didn't seem very likely.

'What was the sound like?' Izzie asked him.

'Sounded like . . . like a giant sneeze.'

'Do squids sneeze?' Izzie asked Eddie. But Eddie didn't know.

No one was quite sure what colour the thing they'd seen was.

'Red.'

'Maybe yellow.'

'Definitely sort of bluey-greenish – like the sea.'

'Black, jet black.'

Eddie overheard one of the teachers telling a reporter what he'd seen.

'I know what I saw and I'm never wrong. It wasn't a whale it was a giant squid. A squid with twenty tentacles.'

The teacher looked so fierce that Eddie didn't like to point out that squids only have two tentacles and eight arms.

'And what did you see?' the reporter asked Eddie.

'A squid,' Eddie said quickly as the teacher nodded. 'A big squid.'

'Eddie!' Izzie said, and when he looked round she beckoned him over.

A girl was holding out her mobile phone. 'It's not a very good picture,' the girl said, 'because my hand was shaking so much.

But it is a picture.' She showed them her phone.

The reporter wanted to see the picture too and then the TV cameras arrived. Eddie and Izzie slipped out.

'What did the photo look like?' Dad asked them as they drove back to the sanctuary.

'It wasn't very clear.'

'You couldn't tell what it was really.'

'Good. Alfonzo was worried about what might happen if the media got hold of the story but without a picture they won't have anything to go on.'

'Did Cornflake come back?' Eddie asked Mum as soon as they got back to the sanctuary.

Mum shook her head.

'I've been calling him,' Toby said. 'From the garden and the front door and our bedroom window.'

'But he's busy playing with his new friends, isn't he?' Mum said, giving Eddie a warning look not to say anything different.

'Yes,' Eddie agreed. 'I bet he's having a lovely time.' He swallowed hard because he wasn't sure about that really. Not sure at all.

'Who's having a lovely time?' Izzie asked, joining them.

'Cornflake,' Mum said, giving her the same warning look she'd given Eddie.

'Oh no,' Beth said, coming into the room. 'Oh no.' She switched on the TV. 'I've just heard something very worrying on the radio in the kitchen.'

They all stared at the television screen in horror. It showed the boat and the children that they'd just come from seeing.

'Now it appears we have our very own creature from the deep in our midst,' the reporter said. 'Something so hideous it gives children nightmares . . .'

'It had tentacles, I tell you,' the teacher Eddie had overheard was saying. 'Hundreds of tentacles!'

The screen filled with scary pictures of sea-monsters.

'Those aren't even real,' Eddie said in disgust. 'They're from films and TV shows.'

'This terrifying Kraken or Leviathan, as creatures like these are also known, must be found . . . ' the reporter continued.

'Oh no,' Izzie said, as the screen filled with helicopters circling above the sea.

'And once it's been found it must be destroyed.'

Now the television showed three men with guns boarding a boat.

'Hunters,' said Beth, as one of them swung his rifle in the air.

'They can't just kill it,' said Mum.

'It hasn't hurt anyone,' said Eddie.

'We have to find it before they do,' Dad said, and at that moment the phone rang.

'There's been another sighting,' Alfonzo said. 'Not far from where it was seen today. Something must be wrong for it to be this close to shore and for there to be this many sightings –'

'Alfonzo, Alfonzo, are you there?' Dad said, when Alfonzo suddenly stopped talking. Outside a storm was coming and there was a crack of thunder and a flash of lightning. 'Alfonzo! Alfonzo!'

But the phone line had gone dead. There was another flash of lightning and the rain started to pour down.

'Would the hunters go after Cornflake too if they saw him?' Izzie asked.

'No,' Dad said. 'Because no one's going to see Cornflake, are they? He's safe here, even if he is living with his friends and not us. He's probably in a cave in the black mountains.'

'I wish he'd come back.'

'Everyone does.'

Toby yawned. Their first full day at the sanctuary had been a very long one.

'Everything will seem better in the morning,' Beth said, as she brought in hot cocoa.

But Eddie didn't see how it could be.

No one wanted to go to bed but Mum said they had to.

'There's nothing we can do at the moment and there's no point you being exhausted in the morning because that won't help anyone.'

Toby was already fast asleep by the time

Mum pulled the covers up over him but Eddie didn't sleep for a long time. He lay with his hands linked behind his head listening to the rain and thinking about the poor creature in the sea and wishing Cornflake would come home.

In her room, Izzie lay wide awake and worrying too, as outside the storm thundered and roared.

CHAPTER 8

The next morning was bright and sunny.

Eddie woke to the sound of a claw tapping on glass and when he opened his eyes he saw it was Cornflake.

The little dragon flapped his wings as he stood on the windowsill and tapped.

'Cornflake!' Eddie cried, and he jumped out of bed to open the window.

Cornflake immediately hopped in and gave a 'caw' of greeting.

'Where've you been?' Eddie said. 'Did you have a good time?'

He could see that the little dragon hadn't been injured. He was just so happy to see him.

Toby was still asleep with his face resting on his teddy. Once he was asleep almost nothing could wake him up until he was ready. But Cornflake managed it.

'What is it?' Toby said sleepily as he rubbed his eyes. But when he saw it was his friend he threw his arms around him. 'Cornflake!' he cried.

Izzie didn't hear Cornflake's taps at the window or her brothers letting him in, but she did see something else. She saw the chicken-parrot, or the dodo called Doris as she now knew it was. Doris was pecking at the grass close to the bush below Izzie's bedroom window.

Izzie crept downstairs, determined to finally say hello. She stopped at the kitchen to make a strawberry jam sandwich before she went out of the front door.

Doris scuttled away into the bush as soon as Izzie came out, but Izzie had expected that. She sat down on the bench that wasn't too far from Doris's bush and not too close to it either. She gave a yawn and pretended to go to sleep while really keeping her eyes open a little bit.

Just as she'd hoped, Doris came closer and then closer still. Eventually the dodo came so close that Izzie could hear it breathing and making a *tuck-tuck* sound in its throat.

'Hello,' said Izzie softly and Doris immediately jumped back. Izzie moved very slowly so as not to startle her again. 'I won't hurt you,' she said. 'Look, I've got food.'

She threw crumbs of the sandwich towards the dodo and at first Doris hopped back, away from the flying food, but then she sniffed and took a step towards the bread and jam. Sniffed again and took another step.

'That's it,' Izzie said. 'That's it.'

Doris opened her beak and the next moment the food nearest to her was gone and then the bit nearest after that and the one after that too.

Izzie smiled.

'Izzie, where are you?' Eddie shouted. 'Cornflake's come back!'

Doris scuttled away into the bush. 'No!' cried Izzie.

Eddie had frightened her.

'I'm sorry, Doris,' Izzie said, and she quickly broke up the rest of the sandwich, dropped it near Doris's bush and ran inside to say hello to Cornflake.

'Cornflake must be really hungry,' Toby said, looking in the cupboard for a bowl. He found a very large one. So big he could pour the whole packet of cornflakes in it.

'That's my cake mixing bowl,' Beth said. But she didn't mind really. Everyone was very pleased to have Cornflake back with them. Even Cornflake couldn't manage to eat a whole packet of cornflakes at once, though.

They were all watching him crunching when the phone rang.

'Turn on the news,' Alfonzo said. His voice cracked as he spoke before he rang off.

Dad switched the TV on.

'And now for some exciting news about the sea-monster that has been sighted off the coast,' the reporter said, and a picture of the hunting boat came on the screen. 'Last night three intrepid hunters were able to locate it.'

The hunters came on the screen. They

were so excited they were all talking over each other.

'It was huge . . . and ferocious . . .'

' . . . tried to rip the boat we were on apart.'

'Fortunately, I got in a lucky shot before the beast could kill us all.'

'And so is the monster dead?' the reporter asked.

The hunters didn't look quite so sure.

'Probably.'

'It screamed in pain so I know I hit it.'

'Got to be dead.'

'There was an awful lot of blood before it sank beneath the waves.'

As the news report ended they all stared at the screen feeling sick. Everyone jumped when the phone rang again.

'There's been another sighting. It's not dead!' Alfonzo shouted down the phone. 'It's to the west of the sanctuary. You might be able to spot it with the telescopes.'

Dad and Izzie ran to the lighthouse. Noah and Eddie hurried to the boat. Toby wanted to go too, but Mum shook her head.

'We'll stay here and play with Cornflake,' she said.

'Do you think he'd like some thyme tea?' Toby asked.

'Do you want some?' Beth asked.

Toby shook his head. 'Cold's all gone now,' he said, picking up his teddy.

As Dad and Izzie headed up the stairs to the top of the lighthouse and the telescopes, Izzie glanced over her shoulder at Dad's office and the map on the wall.

'Hang on a minute, Dad,' she said, as she went into the room.

Izzie looked at the yellow drawing pins on the map showing where the sea monster had been seen so far. It wasn't going in a straight line and it had made lots of twists and turns, but it was definitely making its way somewhere. She stood at the back of the room and squinted at the map.

'Dad. It's coming here!' she shouted.

Dad came running back down the few steps he'd gone up.

'The sea monster's headed to the sanctuary,' Izzie told him. 'It looks like it was always trying to come here.'

'Are you sure?' he asked her.

'Yes – look.'

They got a ball of string and twisted it round each of the drawing pins. It was a winding route. But it was definitely a route or sea path to the sanctuary.

Dad phoned Alfonzo immediately to let him know.

'We think . . .' he started to say.

But Alfonzo didn't let him finish.

'It's coming to the sanctuary!' he shouted down the line.

Dad dropped the phone and he and Izzie raced out of the lighthouse to the beach.

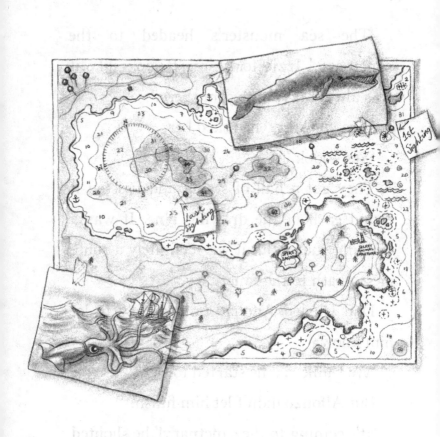

CHAPTER 9

SAS

Down at the beach, Eddie helped Noah push the dinghy out into the sea. The storm from the night before had caused even more driftwood than usual to be cast up on the shore.

'Put this on,' Noah told Eddie, handing him a lifejacket and putting one on himself.

'I haven't been in a dinghy before,' Eddie said, as he climbed in.

'Then make sure you hold on to the ropes,' Noah warned him. 'Don't want you going overboard.'

Eddie held the ropes tightly. He definitely didn't want to land up in the water either.

The waves crashed angrily over the rocks and the dinghy was tossed and turned as they headed out to sea. Eddie shivered and his knuckles turned white. It was cold, much colder out at sea than it was inland.

'Been out in worse weather than this lots of times,' Noah told him and Eddie nodded.

He was starting to feel a bit seasick from all the bumpy waves and he was glad he'd got a lifejacket on. He stared at the rocks ahead and to the sides of them. He was very glad that Noah knew exactly where they were. Then he saw one of the rocks move. He looked again, thinking maybe it was just an illusion caused by the waves. No, there was definitely something there. Something that was the colour of wet rock but not a rock.

'Look!' he said to Noah and he pointed to what he'd seen.

Noah stopped the boat and picked up the binoculars.

'Well I never,' he said.

'What is it?' asked Eddie.

'I don't believe it.'

'What?'

'It looks like a sea serpent, a plesiosaurus in fact. No, wait . . . there's two of them!' Noah started up the boat and headed in the serpents' direction. 'They'll get caught on the rocks like the ships in the olden days if they keep heading that way!'

Eddie couldn't bear the thought of the two water dinosaurs trying to reach the safety of the sanctuary, but not being able

126

to get there because of the rocks. As they got closer he saw that one of them was as big as a whale and the other one was only the size of a baby elephant. The big one seemed to be trying to help the smaller one to keep its head above the water, but the waves were so high it seemed almost impossible. The smaller one looked like it was exhausted and really struggling to keep afloat. It looked very sick.

'We have to help them!' Eddie shouted above the waves. 'We have to do something!'

'You're right,' Noah shouted back. 'But we can't take the baby aboard the dinghy, it's too big – it'd capsize us!'

Eddie grabbed the spare lifebuoy and threw it towards the sea serpents. It was all he could think of. But the waves took the orange ring away from the water dinosaurs instead of towards them.

'Sorry,' Eddie said to Noah, now they'd lost the lifebuoy for nothing.

Noah shook his head. 'It was a good idea,' he called out as he steered the dinghy over to the ring and hooked it out. 'Let's try that again.'

This time Noah steered the dinghy in front

of the sea serpents so that the waves carried the lifebuoy to them instead of away. But Eddie now wasn't so sure his idea had been such a good one after all.

'They won't know that it's there to help them,' he said, but then he watched in amazement as the large sea serpent picked the lifebuoy up in his mouth and dropped it over the small one's head.

'It's Spike!' Noah shouted. 'I'd know him anywhere! Spike's come back and he's got his young 'un with him. Here Spike, grab this.' He threw out a rope and Spike took hold of it with his teeth. Noah steered the dinghy into shore, dragging the two water dinosaurs behind them.

CHAPTER 10

If it's headed here then it knows about this place, Izzie thought as she ran along the beach after Dad. Did all secret animals know about the sanctuary? They couldn't, could they? It didn't seem possible. But somehow, being here, it did seem like it could be true.

'I can see the dinghy,' Dad shouted, and he pointed out to sea. 'They're bringing whatever it is into shore with them.'

'Wait for me!' Toby shouted. He had his teddy with him as he ran towards them.

'Toby, come back!' Mum shouted as she and Beth ran after him along the beach. Cornflake flew above them and out to sea every now and again, cawing loudly.

As the dinghy came closer they saw that it was not one animal but two. A large sea monster was trying to help a smaller sea monster that seemed not to be able to swim any further.

'The small one's hurt,' Izzie said, and she

remembered the hunters and their guns. She hoped it was going to be all right. 'We have to help them.'

The water was now shallow enough for the larger serpent to stand up in and it gave a bellow that could only be a cry for help.

'It's Spike! Oh, Spike, we've missed you so,' Beth cried, as she ran out into the sea to help the giant creature and his child to shore. Dad waded into the sea after her to help and eventually the two sea serpents made it through the shallows and flopped onto the sand. Safe at last.

'Wasn't that a bit dangerous?' Mum said. 'He could have killed you.'

'Not dangerous at all,' Beth told her. 'Spike wouldn't hurt a fly – in fact, he'd probably be frightened of one. I can't believe he swam all this way back to us.'

'I can,' said Mum. 'He's a parent now and even if he doesn't always feel very brave he has to act like he does.'

The small sea serpent lay on the beach gasping for air as its father bellowed again.

'It's all right,' Beth said, patting Spike's long neck. 'It's going to be OK. We'll help your baby.'

Izzie and Dad helped Eddie and Noah to pull the dinghy onto the sand as Alfonzo came running along the beach to join them.

'Spike came back,' Noah told him, and his eyes were all watery. 'He came back because his baby needs our help. But I don't know, I really don't know. I just hope we aren't too late. Poor thing must have got very cold and we could see it was exhausted. It couldn't even keep its head above the water. That's when Eddie had the good idea of throwing it a lifebuoy and we towed them to shore.'

The baby sea monster made a groaning sound followed by a sneeze that sprayed Noah but Noah didn't mind a bit.

'It's going to get well, isn't it?' Izzie said, holding her dad's hand tightly. 'The hunters didn't shoot it?'

The baby sea serpent had to be OK. It had come so far with Spike and braved so much.

'Hard to say yet,' said Alfonzo, kneeling down beside the baby sea serpent. 'It's a young male, and he does look very, very sick. It's strange though, neither of them seem to have been injured by the hunters even though there was definitely blood in the sea in the TV footage.'

The young sea serpent was shivery with cold. Spike did his best to keep his son warm by lying close and wrapping his flippers around him but they could all see that Spike was cold and exhausted too.

CHAPTER 11

'What can we do to help them?' Mum asked, looking at the sea serpents huddled together. 'There must be something we can do. We have to . . .'

'Make them get-better tea,' Toby said.

'Made me all better.'

But no one was listening to Toby.

'I bet they're hungry,' said Eddie.

'And very cold,' said Dad. 'Let's gather up all the driftwood we can find, there's plenty along the shore. They're too big and too tired out to move but a fire will help to keep them warm.'

'We'll get blankets,' said Mum and Beth and they ran back to the cottage to collect some.

Noah and Alfonzo helped to find driftwood too and for a moment no one besides Cornflake was paying attention to Toby as he headed over to the two sea serpents. 'It's OK,' he said. 'You'll be OK. I make you some get-better tea,' he said. Toby left his teddy next to the baby sea monster as he headed back to the herb garden. The little plesiosaurus cuddled into the teddy bear and sighed.

Dad was right about the driftwood. All over the beach there were bits of broken wooden boat hulls, some from years ago, as well as branches of trees and driftwood turned white by the sea and the sun.

By the time Izzie and Eddie came back with what they'd gathered Spike had fallen fast asleep and was making loud snoring sounds.

Eddie grinned at Izzie. They'd laughed at Dad snoring on the minibus a few days ago but that was nothing compared to a sea serpent's snores!

'Right, let's get this fire lit,' Dad said, once the wood was piled up. He struck a match but it went out, as did the second one and the third. Alfonzo cupped his hands around the match, but even when they managed to get the flame to the wood it went out again because of the wind.

Cornflake made a cawing sound and then flew down and landed next to the wood pile.

He breathed out a stream of flames – far more than he'd ever done before – and the driftwood immediately caught light.

'Something he must have learnt from his new big dragon friends,' Izzie said. She looked over at the small sea serpent. He didn't snore as he slept. He made wheezing whimpering sounds and there was a rattling coming from inside his chest.

They all watched him and worried. Hopefully the fire would warm him up.

'I can't bear it – we have to do something else to help them,' Mum said.

'They'll be hungry when they wake up,' Dad said.

'That's it! We'll get them some food ready.'

'Sea kale,' said Noah.

'It was always Spike's favourite food,' said Beth.

Izzie and Eddie ran off to pick some from the garden.

'Anyone seen Toby?' Mum asked, looking round.

'I think he went with Izzie and Eddie,' Noah said.

Mum and Beth headed after them.

'Let's use the wheelbarrow to bring the sea kale back,' Eddie said to Izzie when they reached the garden.

'Good idea.'

They were collecting the sea kale and putting it in the wheelbarrow when Izzie saw Toby pulling up herbs.

'That's not sea kale,' she told her little brother.

'Sea kale looks like cabbage, remember,' said Eddie.

'I know,' Toby said. 'Make get-better tea for Serpy.'

'Who's Serpy?' they asked, puzzled.

'Baby sea serpent,' Toby said, as he headed towards the cottage with his bucket of thyme.

'Toby wants to make the sick baby sea serpent some thyme tea,' Eddie told Mum when she and Beth came into the garden.

Mum looked at Beth. 'Couldn't hurt,' she said, and they both went into the cottage to help Toby make the tea and mix in the honey.

'Tea make Serpy all better,' Toby said, as they carried the tea in a bucket down to the beach.

'He's not used to drinking hot things so

we need to let it cool first,' Mum said, when Toby wanted the little sea serpent to drink it straight away. 'And he's still sleeping. We'll wait until they wake up.'

It didn't take long for Spike to wake up once Eddie and Izzie had tipped the sea kale from the wheelbarrow next to him. His nose sniffed at the air in his sleep, then his eyes opened and next his long neck swung round and his giant jaws opened wide. The sea kale was all gone in a few bites and Spike licked round his mouth with his long tongue and then stared down at the sand and gave a loud sigh, as if he wished that there was some more.

Eddie and Izzie knew what they had to do.

'More sea kale,' said Izzie, and they ran with the wheelbarrow back to the garden.

'Lucky there's lots of it,' Eddie said.

While they were gone the little sea serpent – or Serpy, as Toby had called him – woke up.

'Can I give him his tea now?' Toby asked, and Mum said he could. 'Tastes good,' Toby told Serpy as he held the bucket out to him. 'Make you all better.'

The little sea serpent put his head down and took a sip and then he took a gulp and a few seconds later the thyme tea was all gone.

'He likes it,' Toby grinned.

'Better make some more then,' said Mum, and they headed back to pick some more thyme.

On the way they passed Eddie and Izzie and their wheelbarrow full of sea kale.

'Serpy get better now,' Toby told them. 'He's had get-better tea.'

The little sea serpent also had some of his dad's favourite sea kale before falling back to sleep. Spike ate the rest of it and then had some more that Eddie and Izzie gathered from along the shore.

'Serpy sounds different now,' Izzie said. The dreadful wheezing and rattling sound in his chest had stopped.

Spike covered one of his son's flippers with his own as they dozed on the beach, with the fire lit by Cornflake and blankets from the cottage to keep them warm.

'He's going to be all right, isn't he?' Izzie asked Alfonzo. 'Serpy?'

But Alfonzo only shook his head and looked sad. 'I don't know. If he lasts through the night there's hope. But the truth is he is very sick and still very weak.'

Eddie and Izzie went back to the cottage with Toby and Mum but the rest of the grown-ups spent the night on the beach watching over the water dinosaurs.

CHAPTER 12

Eddie and Izzie ran down to the beach as soon as they woke up the next morning.

'How are they?' Izzie asked.

'Well, they had a good night's sleep.

But they could do with some more sea kale,' Alfonzo told her.

'Coming right up,' said Eddie and he and Izzie headed off with the wheelbarrow to find some. There was almost none left in the garden so they had to pick more of the wild sea kale growing along the beach. Luckily there was lots of it.

Toby and Mum made some more tea for Serpy and the little sea serpent drank it all up then put his head down to Toby so Toby could stroke him.

'He likes that teddy of yours,' said Noah. 'Slept curled up to it all night long.'

'Here we are,' Eddie said, as he and Izzie came back with a wheelbarrow full of sea kale.

Spike's long neck swung over and he dropped half of it in front of Serpy and ate the rest of it himself in two big mouthfuls.

'I told you eating greens is good for you,' Beth told Toby as they watched Spike eating. 'They make you grow.'

Toby looked horrified. 'Don't want to be big as Spike!' he said. 'Be too big for my bed.'

No one wanted to leave Serpy and Spike so Mum and Beth made breakfast for them all at the house and brought it down to the beach.

They spent all the following days at the beach too. Each day Serpy seemed a little better. Spike was back to his normal playful self, and rolled onto his back so Noah could give his tummy a scratch. He even tried playing chase with Eddie and hide and seek with all the children – although he was a bit easy to spot.

Serpy was now looking stronger and eating all the sea kale Eddie and Izzie brought him and his dad. He even managed to stand up and take a few wobbly steps to the sea with the children following him. Spike was so happy he ran round and round in circles.

'He's going to be OK, isn't he?' Izzie asked, and Alfonzo said yes.

That day they had a picnic on the beach to celebrate Serpy's recovery with more sea kale for Spike and Serpy and strawberry jam sandwiches and cakes for everyone else.

Eddie and Izzie went in and out of the water all day playing with Spike. Serpy wanted to join in too but Spike only let him do so for a little while before he pushed him back to the shore.

'He's being a good dad,' said Beth. 'Even though Serpy would like to keep on playing Spike knows his son's not strong enough to do so yet.'

Toby sat with Serpy and Cornflake on the beach and watched Spike and Eddie and Izzie playing in the sea. Serpy held the teddy that Toby had given him under his flippers.

In the sea, Eddie clung on to Spike's neck as Spike stood up. It was a long way down.

'What's that?' said Eddie, pointing at a dark shape far out on the horizon.

Spike looked towards where Eddie had pointed, saw the shape too and bellowed. He swam back to shore, put Eddie carefully down on the beach, dived back into the sea and headed out into the waves towards the rock-coloured shape Eddie had seen.

'What's going on?' Izzie asked.

But Eddie didn't know.

Serpy made small whimpery sounds as if he wasn't quite sure where his dad had gone or if he was coming back. He held on tightly to the teddy and put his flipper in his mouth.

'It's OK,' Toby said, patting Serpy. 'Your dad'll come back. He wouldn't leave you.'

A few minutes later Serpy gave a cry of sheer joy and headed to the sea. Spike was heading back through the waves and there was a second sea serpent with him now.

When they came ashore the new sea serpent wrapped its neck around Serpy's neck and licked his head. Serpy squealed with delight.

'It's his mummy!' Toby said, jumping up and down. 'His mummy came home.'

And Toby was right. As far as Alfonzo could work out, the creature people had thought was a giant squid was not one animal but three – Spike and Serpy's

mother travelling close together as they helped Serpy through the waves.

'Twelve flippers, three tails and three long necks – they would have made a very strange sight indeed,' Alfonzo said. 'No wonder no one knew quite what the mysterious creature was.'

'It was Serpy's mum that the hunters shot,' Dad said. 'And Spike carried on here with his son.'

'Fortunately I can see from here that where she was shot is healing well – although she'll probably always have a scar,' said Alfonzo.

'They wanted to bring their baby back here to the sanctuary so we could help it,' Izzie said.

'And we did,' said Toby.

'Serpy's mum must be starving,' Eddie said, and he and Izzie rushed to fetch more sea kale for their newest arrival.

The two big water dinosaurs wrapped their long necks around each other and then separated so they could both nuzzle their little one.

'Will they stay at the sanctuary now?' Eddie asked Noah.

'Hard to say, but I hope so,' Noah said. 'I really hope so.'

The next day Spike took his family back to the turquoise lake that had been his home before he'd left the sanctuary. Serpy splashed into the water and then rolled over onto his back with his legs in the air while his parents swam beside him.

'Serpy looks comfy,' Toby laughed.

'And very happy,' Mum agreed.

'It's so good to have Spike back,' said Noah.

'So do you still want to leave?' Beth asked Mum. 'It's been almost week.'

Izzie held her breath. But she needn't have worried.

Mum shook her head. 'I never want to leave,' she said. 'The Secret Animal Society's work here at the sanctuary is too important to want to go anywhere else – ever.'

CHAPTER 13

SAS

It was late at night and Izzie was fast asleep when she was woken by a strange sound. A humming of different notes and pitches went on and on and filled the air with sweetness.

Izzie ran downstairs and found Noah

and Beth were already there. The rest of the family arrived to join her. Even Toby had woken up.

'What's going on?' he said.

'Doesn't happen more than once in a blue moon, but when it does you're in for a treat. It's even better when you hear it outside,' Noah told them, as he led them out into the night.

The sound seemed to be coming from everywhere: the sea, the sky, even below the ground.

'It's the song of the sanctuary animals,' Beth told them. 'I think they're saying thank you for what you did, saving the baby plesiosaurus. It always surprises me when people say animals can't communicate. In my experience they always can. All you have to do is watch and listen. Each song and singer is uniquely different.'

Cornflake opened his mouth and joined in with his higher pitched voice. The large dragons flew overhead, their shadows passing over them, and they heard them singing too.

Izzie looked over at Doris's bush and saw that the dodo had come out and was joining in too.

'It's so lovely,' Izzie said, as they stood surrounded by the song in the darkness.

'I never get tired of it,' says Noah. 'And I know you won't either.'

One of the voices was so rich and deep it seemed to almost hum through Izzie from

her toes to the ends of her hair. She knew
it was the sound of Spike and his family
and that Spike the sea serpent was smiling
as he sang.